The
STRUCTURES
COLLECTION

Antonio Magogoli

DYNATOX MINISTRIES
INTERNATIONAL

Borneo – East Brunswick – Reseda

Published by
DYANTOX MINISTRIES INTERNATIONAL
with permission from the Magogoli Estate

http://dynatoxministries.com

ISBN-13:
978-0615989334
ISBN-10:
0615989330

<u>CONTENTS</u>

I shall jump right into things.

Structures are ideally objects that are partially manmade and partially a result of some ill-gotten epiphenomenon. As I write this I am staring off out the window while also gazing at the pile of books on my desk as well as picking a scab on my leg.

So many things fall by the wayside!

Gennaro picks your thoughts and your philosophies out of the trash. He compiles them and puts them away in his burlap sack. He'll have use for them later. He'll turn your words and deeds into sickening dissections of situational complexity which will mean nothing to you but everything to him. That doesn't matter. You'll reap the benefits. Oh, the benefits!

All ill-fated solutions of a man named Aldo who squeezes his redundant machine and exits the room with ink-stained hands. He stands in front of the shop and sets himself on fire.

Gennaro is the only one brave enough to dig through the biological rubble. He finds what he is looking for. He finds the key! What key? Oh, you *know* what key! The key to scholarship and the expansion of the amoral mind. Such things you should know already. You don't own the keys but your entire body is a lock.

Gennaro has climbed mountains but they are *other* mountains if you can grasp my meaning. His comrades were lost in their frostbite and tears. Even the mayor lost his life when he gazed upon the creeping fury in the alcove high up on the mount.

Some many structures fall by the wayside. Your words flake off like scabs. Like scabs!

You receive blades for holidays. The men don't move under your command. They meet resistance. Their egos deflate on the shore and create the beach where the caves begin to appear.

You are seething. You return to your birthplace. You wish for the ideal. You sell dead fruit to dead men. And they eat! The dead men eat! They eat dead men!

Who will iron your clothes? Who will iron the socks you will wear up the cliff? You won't know cobblestones. You only know devils.

Gennaro brings you good tidings and breaks glass over the heads of cheating spouses. Be careful! He is turning the corner and will come by your window with a suitcase full of several horrible murders. Because of them, I have had several seizures. The relationship between the crimes and my bodily disruptions is something mysterious and most likely preternatural in origin. I cannot prove this, of course, but I looking for the cause and am making that search the focus of my current placement in life.

Gennaro knows about the murders. This I know.

He sighs between the beatings he gives me. He bruises me for hours and hours until my body is a dark blob of dark blue dawn. My bloated little head is fodder for his curious anger. He wants to operate on my psyche. His fists are scalpels. He will be my doctor!

The village I grew up in has been overrun by poisonous crops and madmen masquerading as corrupt politicians. I haven't voted in years. There is no use in doing so. All the votes are burned in a mass bonfire in the midst of a chaotic civil demonstration. Beatings! Decapitations! Rape! Political speeches! There is no use in going back to the village. I feel no need to do so.

The folk songs of my village are haunting odes to the Stone Age perversions of my ancestors.

> **You are the only one in the universe.**
> **Eat the false moon.**
> **Drink wine unearthed from the caves.**
> **The stench of cosmic pride.**
> **Your intestinal homesteads relieve you.**
> **You wear masks and make noise.**
> **Sing your songs but don't worry.**
> **The solar crocodile opens wide.**

He eats and talks French and he is the surgeon! He wants to render his fantasies into meat. He is a whore on the beach of philosophical pondering, a devil from deep in the earth, from the bottle, from the wet spider web of the north shaped into triangles and draining into rotted childhoods vomited back into political art of his teenage years.

Things won't go the way of his philosophy if he doesn't put on the shoes, put on his father's worn shoes and watch the trucks go by with their sheep and their ugly stink of men, perhaps police officers perhaps just farmers waiting for blood and plebian genes.

Things will not get better, dear Gennaro. Things will get much, much worse and spill the blood of millions in the caves off the coast, the caves filled with warlocks and bottles of filthy lungs and spells and teeth but we do not believe in these things, these ugly things because the last thing we want to do is accept the superstitions of our mothers and long faded shadows blacking out windows and ugly skin we want to strip off and shade the sky with. Gennaro doesn't deserve us.

Everything is dirty and corrupt within the village and outside of it. We have no energy for anything but our silly philosophy. We have no energy for anything but some form of hate for every form of life and life's meanings that are splattered through the minds of simple skulls. Blood from wounds shower us. Into the cave with you, Gennaro! You look at me so oddly as if I'd betray your philosophy or betray your somewhat incomplete life in that hospital. What a hospital it is!

All the nurses prod you. All the doctors examine you with their spidery fingers and metallic instruments. They fill out charts in cuneiform and call upon your parents to tell them the terrible news.

Gennaro is contagious!

What's wrong with your pillow? It's lumpy and it smells like burnt hair. It is shaped like a triangle and it is on the table. It is sick. It has a virus. You're eating a meal of raw meat and potatoes. You should be painting the walls. You should be extending an invitation to your friend, the priest.

What a good idea you have!

That Aldo fellow is someone you simply cannot trust. Why do you insist on letting him paint your portrait? He is a person you simply cannot trust!

Her raw primeval mound is a pound of flesh, quite a sight to behold. It resembles a beaked clown. Our ancestors slaughtered plenty of clowns in their day, clowns in gowns, clowns that were drowned, simply to give flesh to the stregheria.

I remember driving my father's car into the field and praying for some sort of return to the earth. What kind of return could I have hoped for? Maybe a return to the hollowness inside? Certainly the planet is hollow. Certainly it is inhabited by those small men I've read about in my father's journals. They sing to certain people, they sing songs and bring so much to them in the corners of mirrors, where you could almost see them. They appear as clowns. They appear as smiling men but are really miserable shells.

Underneath my bed I have a collection of ivory wands. Most of them are from the 19th century but I have one that dates back to the 16th century. Several frogs have been used in construction of these wands. They are like canes except that they consist of a more potent motive for action.

BEHOLD THE MAN

It has come to my attention that several sources have degraded my reputation. This cannot stand as is and must be fixed in any way possible.

This cult of corrupt men who pervert the name of my sister and her concrete garden, well, these are men who deserve two deaths!

You know their leader, this man named Aldo De Luca, cousin of Marco Del Duca, and father of the infamous man known simply as *"THE INMOST HOST."*

I know where you can find these men. They hide out in the back room of the shop called Aegean Okra. I've been there. I know many of you have been there. It is a den of vipers. The birthplace of Chelphun! That fickle light bringer.

It has come to my attention that several sources have

There are rituals inherent in structures, simple structures, complex structures, all structures alive or dead, beautiful or ugly, calm or anxious, shoved into dust, those cement structures and structures made of playing cards and popsicle sticks, twigs and matches, idols and fermented fruit. Your lemon tree is for the hangman. You turn your radio into an instrument....for torture!

I have met with men on trains and have divulged the secrets concerning all structures and have opened my EYES for them. They inserted their visions and philosophies into my BRAIN.

Everyone knows the sodomites run the villages up north. What a cesspool of laws and liberation all twisted into semen-stained ropes hanging from lemon trees and overlooking their concrete structures, giving the villagers something to look at when they are raped with books and witch-wine, bottles of clear depravity fermented from the testicles of happy men, eight-hundred proof and all with conspiracies of local elections, those bastard sodomites!

I BEHELD HIM

SUICIDE

As well
At
In the nighttime
Will commit acts of rape
Rimbaud was a bore
Relives it all
He thinks
Selvansl Tularias
PACHA
Goes
Shopping
And
Picks up a silk suit
It fits him quite nicely
PACHA
In the countryside
He is a deviant beyond
All deviance
But don't we all
Burning his ugly papers
PACHA
And comes close to

The diagnosis, of course, was more severe than I had expected. 'He is, no doubt, mentally ill,' they had told me. I was writing on the stone walls, eating roots and seeing visions, telling the other villagers about those visions, causing dreams, causing a culture to form, shaping attitudes, routines of sex, commerce, astronomical contradictions. What should I have expected?

Ill-fated solutions, I'd say. In shackles I still write books.

I see a picture of a camel and I have the urge to rip the animal apart and devour it, not out of a desire for sustenance but out of pure hate for that satanic desert creature, the camel, that ugly thing.

I see their pictures, their photographs, and I put them on the floor, stomp on them, spit on them, urinate and defecate on them and worse! I do things that God closes His eyes to because He knows it would corrupt even Him.

He doesn't stop me, no, He doesn't stop me because He knows it is out of my own Free Will that I do these things and He created this Free Will or rather, He allowed this Free Will to reign in the hearts and souls of ugly men like myself so He closes His eyes and thinks of pure things while I desecrate the images of men and women who arouse my hateful pineal gland.

Gennaro knows my deep secrets and records them on his tape recorder. He blackmails me daily. I am not making this up. I am not creating stories for further alibis or extensions of my own philosophies or fantasies or written descriptions of my nervous tension. The entire structure created with my feverish paranoia has toppled.

I will leave Bernhard Province and will never speak of it again. This I know. This I can promise you. Tell S. D'Antona that I have no more use for his silly myths.

Gennaro wishes to slit throats in his dreams. Do you ever dream?

He wishes to watch the dream-blood ooze in that special way one only sees in dreams…the slow oozing…the slow movement that tingles the body and relieves the mind of all tension and worry. Do you ever worry?

He wishes to slaughter indiscriminately because that's what his philosophy calls for…even in dreams. Yes, even in dreams. Do you think dreams are premonitions? Do you believe dreams are important for a person's soul?

Gennaro writes and writes and yet…he never does not feel satisfied. But who is ever really satisfied? Who really ever feels content in this life? No one! No one feels content and so when you tell me you feel so satisfied, I know you are a liar!

Let's cut to the heart of the matter, shall we?

There comes a time in each generation when one individual must vent their grievances and grief and dissatisfaction and spiritual anger and lustful anguish in the form of the written word.

Your hymns will no save you. All desire for revenge or recuperation is overshadowed by your lust for literary exposure. Gennaro laughs at such dreams! He has no such dreams. He has no dreams at all!

CHAPTER ONE

The ink has been harvested from the veins of the village harlot. It has been harvested from the obsidian rain that falls over the village orphanage. It has been harvested from the candles that stand guard over the village's black masses. It is the ink of fallen faces…and of *DEATH*!

Gennaro cracks open the bottle filled with bile and broad strokes of old pens and finally, oh finally, the lapdogs of the mayor are slit from ear to ear. Gennaro laughs and pockets the knife.

He'll write his manifesto tonight. Yes, tonight! Then and only then will the people know his venom and his painful extraction. He will turn all structures into awful pools of resentment.

WHAT
MUST
WE
DO
TO
PREVENT
GENNARO
FROM
UNLEASHING
HIS
WRATH
UPON
THE
WRITTEN
PAGE
?

First draft:

The housing project is the only structure I liked in the entire city of Turin. The cement and glass structure is known as LOLLOBRIGIDA and was named after the actress Gina Lollobrigida. It was built in 1968 by Renato Questi, an architect and entrepreneur from Florence. Questi originally made his fortune publishing religious tracts in Slavic. He became an architect after having seen Marco Bertolucci's 1959 film STRUCTURES.

The film was Bertolucci's last before he left the film industry for a career in architecture. Most film critics were saddened by the loss of such a visionary.

STRUCTURES was unlike any film of its day. Audiences were not ready for such an artistic display. Holger Karoli of Cine Italia X said the film was "the closest thing to watching architecture as actors, a quasi-surrealist film without all the pretentiousness. A true delight for both the eyes and the mind. I can never look at manmade structures the same way again."

The housing project where I stayed is the only place I ever felt safe. That probably was not by accident. It was the only place I've ever known where I did not get beaten by the circumstances of my arrival. I really am just a poor example of urban youthfulness. Look at me.

HORRIBLE STRIKE THE CURRENT SEIZURES SIGH BEATINGS AND HOURS SOME OTHER THEY WERE LOST IN TEARS CREEPING FURY THE LOST HIS LIFE IN PROSE **DEAR** LORDS AND THOSE AREN'T GAMES, MY DEAR FELLOWS, KNIVES OF MOUNTAIN CLIMBERS AND HOISTING UP RUINS FOR J. PARSON'S ABORTIONS IN ROME EVERYTHING MOTHERHOOD FEELS STRAINED AND SPRAINED **TOILET** MOUNTAINS LOST TO MURDERS THE OF STRIKING TURTLE SHORES IN THE TRIANGLE BETWEEN RESTAURANT ATE WITH **MISTRESS** AND BOTTLED UP BOXES **WE'RE** NOT PRINTING THE LAST OF HIS WORDS WE ARE **NOT** PRINTING THE LAST OF HIS EVIL VILE PHILOSOPHY WE DO NOT MAYOR SUPPORT ANY WORDS AND OH THOSE 'ORRIBLE LADIES AND 'URDERS OV BRUISED 'UMOUR AND BLACK LICE SAINTHOOD BLEEDING BIRTHDEATH AND **DAMNED** WITHOUT WHICH **WE** WOULD NOT **HAVE** PURPLE THIS SUCH PHILOSOPHY RETURNING OURSELVES TO THE GARAGE WITHOUT OF OUR **PITIFUL** PAINFUL SPITTING AND TRAINING IN THE MIDST OF THE VILLAGE EPIDEMIC **PRAYERS** LIKENED TO DUST AND HANDS RIPPER TRADE STREET ROUGH THINGS

Here is the story of Gennaro. Pure and simply I shall explain my experiences with the prick. I've reached the point where I cannot go one mile without someone asking me about my experiences and though it sickens me to have to explain myself, I shall have to do so in order to keep what little sanity I have left in my grasp.

Gennaro was born in one of the poorer villages south of here. The exact village is unknown, of course, since the villages down there keep no records for births or deaths and Gennaro himself would not divulge that information to anyone. I do know he was born in one of the poorest of villages. His mother was most likely a prostitute who worked the beach, waiting for the fishermen to come in. His father, from what I know, was unemployed but made some money selling secondhand newspapers.

Gennaro's childhood was spent helping his father dig through trash as well as taunting the other village children. He was a well-known thief and firebug by the time he was twelve years old though no one sought any formal charges against him seeing that his mother was a prostitute and his father was a pathetic example of a parental figure. In fact, most of the villagers felt sorry for poor Gennaro.

By the time he was fifteen, he graduated to more vicious crimes but none I feel comfortable speaking about. They disturb me to no end especially since Gennaro himself gave me detailed accounts of each crime complete with crumpled photographic evidence and written journals (though the writing itself was such as you'd expect from an eight year old because Gennaro never did attend school).

At age eighteen, Gennaro traveled north which is where he and I met. I was working at a small lending library and I had caught him stealing an atlas.

I am but a simple structure caught in a complex plan created by a simple god who does not know that structures can't mix.

(Structures) II.
SUCH WORDS

We need no black or white magic here. We need no guns or poison. We need no political intrigue or domestic strife. We have enough black hearts to satisfy the devil for a hundred years.

Pardon my vulgar language but: *it's all bullshit*.

Every structure I've buried in my career...Gennaro has resurrected!

Bullshit all day and all night. Such a silly way to live. Such a silly way to die! Buried under concrete! Buried under cement! Buried under office buildings, houses, all sorts of devilish things!

SUCH VULGAR LANGUAGE
FOR SUCH A VULGAR YOUNG CIVIL
SERVANT
WHY DON'T YOU CRAWL BACK INTO
THAT HOLE
YOU CALL YOUR MOTHER

Every village is a hellhole with all these ugly buildings with their ugly doors. Ugly wood for ugly faces. They hide in the cellars like rats. They hide in the shadows like defrocked priests. Their hands are equally guilty of unholy touching. These structures are ours for the demolishing.

Pardon my uncouth language but: *it's all bullshit*.

You live in such a silly way. I think you should be buried under your bullshit. I think you should be buried under your housing projects. I think you should be buried, buried, buried.

Documentation: *Chamsin Soundtrack*

A slight ringing in the ears.
The sound of rain upon dirt.
Tin cans blowing against wooden doors.
Bicycle chains in need of grease.
Necklaces falling into mud.
Bone bending and then cracking.

A headache.

halluzination strategies that are scratched into vinyl. There's nothing Gennaro can do to stop us. You cannot and will not prevent me from going through with my endeavor. What endeavor? Haven't you been listening? You are quite deaf when you want to be! I don't understand your reluctance to understand me even under the circumstances I still think I make a lot of sense despite your **nonsensical** nodding and babbling as if you really are quite deaf as a result of your father's boxing you upon the ears and even though I have some sympathy for you, I cannot condone your intentional ignorance or rather the appearance of ignorance (because I do know you understand me, yes I do, even though you stare at me with such a dumbfounded look, your face all blubbery and pale and scarred from those childhood diseases) that you use to avoid the problem at hand, the problem that hinders me from creating this vinyl record of my **experiments**, my philosophies concerning my long awaited cure for all earthly, humanist and psychological vaccinations originating in the village north of here, the village where **you** lived for a short time while preparing your own thesis for your university, the university that expelled you despite your high scores because you were **never** one to conform to all manners of decorum and behavior and **thought** processes that weren't purely a result **of** your own experimentation in the laboratory of your halluzination strategies that are scratched into vinyl.

"Sto cercando Gennaro!"

Il bagnato i ragazzi vivono nel paese. Il wet rane gridano nel fiume. Il wet macchine parlare nero estivo. La casa è umida. La casa è insetti. Voi siete qui. IO sono qui. È il mio occhio nero. Si blocca il mio occhio. Si bagna la mia casa. La pioggia è bagnato. La pioggia è rane. Le macchine sono le rane. Le macchine sono nere e le rane. Dove è Gennaro?

L'estate è nero e blu. L'estate è vomito rana. L'autunno è il rumore. Il tuo viso è il rumore. Il tuo volto è nero village. La malattia è ragazza. Il fango è forte. Il caffè è pianeta. Nascondi il tuo volto. Nascondi la tua pelle. Si pompa il pneumatico. Siete stanchi.

È ritardato. È malato. Sei un debole rana. Il vomito e merda vomita. La gamba è pieno. I miei testicoli sono fatti di vetro. Camminate nella luna. Si trova fuori la luna. Si mangia la luna. Lei vomita sulla luna. Lei vomita la luna.

Ci sono trasmissioni telefoniche vomito. Sei un bianco sole fiore culto. Si mangia il fiore. Il vomito urine auto. È falso il tuo volto. Fumate insetti prodotti chimici. Mangiate Gennaro. È possibile utilizzare pelle coperte. Lei vomita rane e mangiare plancton nel villaggio. Non ti piace sentire la tua voce che vomita. Si argento vomito.

Guarda che cosa ho fatto. Attenzione a ciò che ha ucciso. Guarda l'assassino vomito in bocca alla sua vittima. Hai un tè? Avete delle rane? Avete gli occhi? MI vomito rane. IO sono automobile merda. MI bloccano il sole in bianco e nero vesti e planetari vomito figg. Si sentono voci di rumore pioggia. Mangio droga diventi giallo e coltello gambe prostituta.

Dove è Gennaro? Quel bastardo ha preso la mia faccia. Quel bastardo ha scritto libri sul mio lungo nero. Si spacca lo specchio nel vomito gli occhi e la crema di rane fuori l'anarchico globo. Il mio amore per te è più grande di suini fango e vomito macchine di pagine di libri, alcuni principe nel villaggio dormire con corpo. Vi chiedo ancora una volta dove è Gennaro?

Toxicological Whispering

There is a minotaur in the traummaschine.

Uli Popp broke Gennaro's chair.

Questo è ciò che l'apocalisse sembra!

A woman chewing on a lollipop stick.

Poor old golem.

White monk's clock.

Il monaco muore nel sangue e vomito fiori di
arcobaleno bestie.

Poor old Gennaro.

White road ash.

Tagliare il bastard's gola!

Inspirate la peste.

Amen

Amon

You're not going anywhere you son of a bitch. You won't get away with this. You think your village will protect you, oh no, my friend. Your throat will be slit nonetheless and your blood shall turn seeds into flowers and corpses into plants with all the little animals singing, "Oh popol vuh! Help us, help us!" as they are thrown into the slaughtering pool and you watch helplessly as your precious books are cut open to reveal the Gammastrahlen-Lamm instructions! Oh you little killer you little gentle sweet young thing who knows everything and bleeds your little face until BLACK BLACK BLACK VOMIT spills into your church head like a poor person's village reflection into mirrors and some hearing device, some self-destructive device Si ereditano i worm e gli occhi neri dei vostri padri e madri e gli zii e le loro automobili e strutture che si sgretolano e strutture che puzzano e si muore come un cane in via del borgo.

CHAPTER 1

Oh, such delight the man had… stalking around the windows of the farmhouse, watching the women undress, watching them sniff their own undergarments, oh, such a particular delight the man feels! His satanic genital stir and it is not unlike the feeling of smothering those animals the previous year.

The old woman he is watching…her bulbous mammary glands, all hefty and pale, swinging like deformed cow udders, oh, the man thinks about slipping a knife into them and watching the gold spill out. What does this man know of such things? How does he know?

He knows because…he is Gennaro!

There is another woman, a bit younger than the older one, and she is sniffing her undergarments, sniffing the crotch until the fabric is worn thin, sniffing the fragments of her own spoiled, soiled self. Oh, Gennaro masturbates against the wall below the window and rubs his prick against the house, scraping skin off and ejaculating into egoless bliss while the young woman licks her undergarments and passes gas because she does not think anyone is watching her. Oh, but Gennaro is watching her! He hears her! He devours her with his mind!

The woman bends over and checks underneath her bed. It is where she keeps her collection of ivory wands. Most of them are from the 19th century but she has one that dates back to the 16th century. Several frogs have been used in construction of these wands. They are like canes except that they consist of a more potent motive for action. Again she passes gas while her posterior is facing the window Gennaro is looking through while he masturbates again through several raw and bleeding orgasms.

He has now created his bitter philosophy!

He has now decided to tear down this pitiful farmhouse!

No structures are safe from our hero!

Nothing is safe!

Nothing!

There are rituals inherent in structures, simple structures, complex structures, all structures alive or dead, beautiful or ugly, calm or anxious, shoved into dust, the inmost host shudders, picked apart by those vicious political vultures, oh those damn bastards! And those cement structures and structures made of playing cards and popsicle sticks. Finally relenting, his father tied a vine around his pitiful organs and splattered something fierce across the field, that southern field, the one with the crosses and the women crying to Mary, the one where the priest had violated that slave. Tutte le strutture sono sbagliate. Gennaro eats the bread and hopes for the worst of things. He always hopes for the worst. A genetic and cultural conflict boards the train from here to Palermo but…there is no train! Those words he scrawled into his mother's white and green body, he squeezed the last remaining remarks from her throat and rendered her useless in the scheme of things. And he does it for you. They occupy an intellectual void like all universities. They don't listen to their elders. We are left home to twaddle and destroy anything and everything, our dreams and illusions of black glass, those buildings we dream of and the buildings we drive by on our way to the slaughter pits, the houses of pungent blood and menstrual fascination. He has ink and king's blood and he has paper and he has time. Oh, does he have time. He has time to make maps of his intellect, diagrams of the cold hells of his lineage, that cursed line of whores and bastards and cutthroats and pederasts and devil worshippers. He will strip his mind of distractions and relinquish control to the brutal airs of his history, his philosophy. The ink has been harvested from the veins of the village harlot. It has been harvested from the obsidian rain spilling, the spit that falls over the village orphanage. It has been harvested from the candles that stand guard over the village's black masses. It is the ink of fallen faces…and of death. He does it for you, the reader of obscene books. I beg to differ, Gennaro. You will not convince me. You will not convince me like you've convinced my comrades. They are ignorant men, ignorant swine, sons of festering whores, of ugly and dying soldiers, and I am not them. So you cannot convince me, you cannot put your stamp onto my soul. You own soul smell likes the inside of satan's fish market, dirty and eternally evil and pungent and you will not bring me into it. No, Gennaro, you will not. I beg to differ. He does it for you, teller of gruesome tales. He does it for you, violator of machines. He does it for you, father of the disturbed and mother of the crippled and diseased and unearthly. He does it for the universe, that brittle and corrupting whore. Gennaro throws marbles against the wall and wishes for them to turn into eyes, small child-eyes, tiny mirrors to the future but he's left disappointed for they are not child-eyes, they are not tiny mirrors to the future. They are simply marbles. No marbles are simple. Marbles are eyes. Marbles follow me

33

and I hate them! They look like cat's eyes. They looks like eyes of little people who invade my room at night while I try to sleep, try to sing, try to count the dreams in my head, try to erase the rapes from my tiny little brain, try to connect the dots of all my books and my records. Gennaro's words are pulled from his teeth, from his mind, from his crackling brain and then, then what? He laughs and pockets the knife! The knife is in his pocket! Do you not understand? Tutte le strutture sono sbagliate. Do you not understand the implications of this pure fact? I dare you to ponder this! I dare you to peruse the words that are floating in the air around Gennaro's head! There comes a time in each generation when one individual must vent their grievances and grief and dissatisfaction and spiritual anger and lustful anguish in the form of the written word. Men, women, children…all were victims of Gennaro's elaborate suicidal purge and urge to kill or stalk the streets and the restaurants that are open far too late where the women dine and drink wine and wait for some sort of ugly fate to come to them. They will curse the day they started menstruating! He has collected their death masks and has taken photographs of their mouths as they whispered their last words, their last shot at entering the heaven of their village's god. Oh, and Gennaro loves those last words. Last words that are carved upon some prick's house, some piece of wood in the woods. How sweet they are in the grey matter of his awful brain! His awful godless cave! There are bats! There are oysters filled with sperm and grim oceanic soup! He enjoys the feel of the weapon in his pocket. In his pocket he also has many other things: chewing gum, bullets, phone numbers of nurses, dirt and dust and stones and bits of a watch. You'd think you'd know better by now. But you don't! You sit here with your wine and your grin and your stupid wife and you think you have my fate in your hands but you do not! Oh, you ugly cow! Oh, you demonic machinist! You think of one thing and do another. I will deconstruct your structures and rebuild myself. I have a gift. The gun. It hums against his leg. It hums in the dead language of murdered children. Gennaro hums along with the knife and remembers cracked teeth and bloated gums. Gennaro's words are pulled from his teeth, from his mind, from his crackling brain and then, then what? He laughs and pockets the knife! The knife is in his pocket! Do you not understand? Do you not understand the implications of this pure fact? I dare you to ponder this! I dare you to peruse the words that are floating in the air around Gennaro's head! Gennaro's hands are not his hands! Gennaro's words are not his words! Gennaro enters the room, enters the piss-poor chamber where he will construct his awful philosophy. After years of blackening the community with his words, Gennaro will build a testament to his ideas. This testament will be a testament to the structures he despises. He will form things, awful things. He will author volumes of his vile philosophy. Those volumes will burn in a library of obsidian cement. As if there is such a thing! He will blanket the world with his mania. Gennaro sings black-hearted hymns and offers up his skin. All the people lit fires of figures, all semi-human but all also totally unlike their counterparts even with the fish markets being what they are, with all the clams and oysters and semi-fresh fish, enlightened eaters, the black faces pinched, all the priests who shop and try to get their fish for free because their boss is the boss and fish should be free, god knows it, and so all of us lose some of our value, just semi-human rungs on a black ladder, a different type of family tree. You want to hammer the nails into the building but you are too afraid to see what comes out of the holes once they are made and you can hear the subtle call of your mother but your mother has been dead for several years and maybe even centuries because you really have no mother but the earth whore who shat you out in the field south of your village. Gennaro, that papal hound, that worshipper of an antiquated Dagon, the pitiful writer of rumors and insidious gossip...he sits alone in his chamber, contemplating the philosophies of ugly reputations. Gennaro wishes to slit throats in his dreams. Slow motion film stock blood village. He wishes to watch the dream-blood ooze in that special way one only sees in dreams...the slow oozing...the slow movement that tingles the body and relieves the mind of all tension and worry. He wishes to slaughter indiscriminately because that's what his philosophy calls for...even in dreams. Yes, even in dreams. It is not a simple task to sum up the events that led to the dissolution of the Bernhard Province. Many writers more intelligent than I have tried (and failed) to come up with an accurate chronology of the events. This is an insane endeavor. Writing is for fools who cannot speak. Cowards! This isn't from any fault of their own but is a result of the intricacy and chaotic nature of the province itself. Both the physical landscape as well as the cultural and political structures were based upon a primitive mythology that was not overtly recognized among the populous and only that fact only manifested itself after the discovery of the personal papers of Antonio D'Antona. It was after that discovery that the true structure of Bernhard Province came to light. Last night, Gennaro dreamt of a camel. The animal was standing in front of him in the desert. They were the only living things for miles until a herd of sheep ran through the scene and large black ships shaped like smiles flew through the air. Gennaro kicked the camel and the animal spoke to him in fluid French. Gennaro couldn't understand the thing. No one can understand the psychological mechanisms responsible for these structures. He kicked it again and the sand gave way and a storm created a face shaped like the camel only larger and more sinister looking. Ugly devils in ivory shapes. A caravan of sick men road up behind Gennaro and asked him if he was willing to sell the camel for they were hungry for camel meat and wanted to devour the thing from front to back and were willing to pay a good price for the beast. Gennaro told the men that he wasn't even sure it was his camel but that he'd be willing to part with it for just some water and maybe a few minutes with the most attractive of the men. One of the men (the youngest) agreed to spend some time with Gennaro and the other men took the camel while Gennaro and the young man sat on the desert sand and started exploring each other's bodies with hand and tongue and finally cock until the camel was slaughtered at which time both men ejaculated into each other's palms after which they drank water and feasted on camel meat and Gennaro awoke with his tongue lapping up the green water on the stone floor. The stones were taken from a pyramidal structure discovered south of the village in 1875 by Aldo Ridolldi. The excavation was not an easy one. The mayor of the village did everything in his power to prevent Ridolldi from unearthing the structure. In the mayor's eyes, it belonged to the village (which by proxy meant it belonged to him, the mayor) and Ridolldi had no right to dig up the mysterious structure despite his having gotten the appropriate permits from the provincial authorities. In this situation, the mayor's approval was no necessary but that didn't stop the mayor from disapproving and doing all he could to curtail Ridolldi's project. In the mayor's eyes, nothing was allowed to be done without his approval and by approval, of course I mean some sort of bribery as that was the way it went in the village and in the province. If Ridolldi had known this, he might have very well greased the mayor's palm but he did not know this and so he went about excavating the pyramidal structure without the permission of the mayor and without the unofficial permission that would have made his job a whole lot easier. But luckily everything worked out in the end and the mayor suffered a heart attack while trying to wrestle some tools away from Ridolldi himself. The poor mayor died holding a small brush used to wipe away dirt from valuable artifacts. Poor Ridolldi hadn't the heart to pry the tool out of the mayor's dead hand and so the man was buried with it and Ridolldi was forced to buy another rather inferior brush for his purposes but really, in the end it all worked out fine for him and for us. Tutte le strutture sono sbagliate. Without structures, we can be free from all forms of psychological warfare and political malfeasance.

Let's reexamine ourselves, shall
we?
So far, so good.

You think so?
I know so.
You are a bastard.

I'm sure that's quite accurate.

It is?
At this point in time, yes.

That's quite introspective.
No, it is not.
Are you Gennaro?
No, I am not.
Then I am Gennaro.

He and I will dine by the window tonight. It will be as pleasant as our psychology allows. I hope to convince him of my sanity. I also hope to convince him of his own. Wish me luck!

Our conversation will most likely disintegrate into a crass discussion about memories of mammary memories and locked doors with keys of vice and specters. He and I will build some structures of speech, structures that will form the epitome of our reconstructive hand devices, the devices we will use to construct parallel structures in the area south of the village, the village where he was born and near the farm where he met his mentor, the mentor that was executed for his bizarre political views, the views that spread like wildfire throughout the surrounding villages despite the attempts by the authorities to silence those philosophies.

Oh, he and I will *potrete cenare con possibili motivi brutto e farfalle!*

I should have known.

such suicidal black-outs are no more.
picking the fruits of our laborious animals.
for the hospital releases us
from some unearthly bondage
without which we
would never know our faces
as they reconstruct
All

INSNIFFEROUS HOSTS

Aldo A. Magogoli

Characters

Paters: An elderly cobbler who lives one of the caves outside of the village.

Aves: The apprentice of Paters. He is also a specter.

Setting

A village in the Bernhard Province.

> *(Lights go out. Curtains go up. The audience sees a small row of dilapidated houses. Paters is walking slowly across the stage while Aves trails behind him, floating..)*

AVES: Ma questo paese vuole uccidere lei, sir!

PATERS: And you think I don't know this! Idiot!

AVES: Scusi, ingegnere.

PATERS: You should be.

> *(Paters and Aves stop at one of the buildings which has a large sign that reads PERVERSIONE NEU OROLOGI.)*

PATERS: *(looks back at Aves)* This is the place? You are sure of it?

43

AVES: SO nel mio cuore che questo è il posto che cerchiamo. IO non

sono per voi, il mio padrone. La vecchia strega sulla spiaggia mi ha detto questo è il posto giusto per acquistare i film di vecchi riti e le macchie solari.

PATERS: It better be!

YOU HAVE BEEN INVITED TO
A SPECIAL EVENT

OH-OM-OHM INTL. PRESENTS
*"Tutte le strutture sono bastioni di nero la
stregoneria"*

Featuring the first performance of

ANTONIO MAGOGOLI
&
HIS PALE KING ORCHESTRA

NARRATOR:

We break away from our childish things.

Even with our head in adult matters, we sometimes feel the need to delve into our past, into our cavernous and ritualized visions of paternal apocalypses. Yes, even Gennaro will take part in our psychological exorcism.

Near the gas station there is a limestone bookshelf full of archaic tomes. What are these books about? I do not know the specifics but I have heard rumors about ugly pale sigils and architectural necromancy.

There is no stupidity worse than death.

We break away from our childish thoughts and routines. I will do nothing again, I will repeat nothing, I will receive nothing.

Di gusto come vita strutturale!
LOOK
 AT
AT
 BROKEN
THE
 EGG
MIRRORS
 GENTLEMAN
BROKEN
 STRUCTURE
INTO
 INTO
EGG
 TRUE
SHELLS
 LOOK
SPOKEN
 THE
LIKE
 SPECTER
A
 OF
TRUE
 MIRRORS
GENTLEMAN
 BROKEN
SPECTER
 SPOKEN
OF
 LIKE
STRUCTURE
 SHELLS

Oh, that devious bastard! Philtrum! Oh, that malicious Gennaro! He will slit your throat while you sleep, while you milk your ugly cows! You commit several crimes but Gennaro has committed hundreds more! He is a legend and a curse!

But what proper procedure is there for dealing with such a devil? I shall tell you. I shall tell you the procedure for dealing with this man, this scoundrel Gennaro!

Your hearts are hard. Your skulls as well. You build yourself another one. It is your co-skull. It is your haven, sanctuary. It is your confessional.

Gennaro plants bombs in your co-skull. He lights the fuse...He spills innocent blood. But for what purpose? *What purpose?*

There is no rhyme, no reason, no melody, no structure to what he does. He does what he does and he blames everyone. He blames the innocent murderer on his death bed. He blames the innocent rapist in the shadow of the obelisk. He blames the innocent hunter eating the bones of his prey.

There is humor to this all, I assure you. Some devious bastards know no bounds. Some devious and malicious structures reincorporated into a bundle of burning bushes and faces, some overheated yeast in the shape of cockle bread.

There are no buildings for your fire.

Dear Gennaro, you are doomed!

BLACK ROMAN GLYPHS

Philtrum left his cigarette burning on the nun's backside. He melted the gold and made a crown. He threw the crown into the river and talked to the fish. The nun did burn, too.

Philtrum broke the chair within the Christian home, a structure of pitiful rot and Anglican foreboding. He reigns from heaven above and burns, too.

Philtrum lights the candle and eats the flame over the blueprints to his structure. He does not burn.

Si gusto strutturali come la morte!

....receive blades for holidays. My bloated little head is fodder for his curious anger. They meet resistance. Their egos deflate on the shore and create the beach where the caves begin to appear. This cannot stand as is and must be fixed in any way possible. I do things that God closes His eyes to because He knows it would corrupt even Him. He sighs between the beatings he gives me. It has come to my attention that several sources have degraded my reputation. He bruises me for hours and hours until my body is a dark blob of dark blue dawn. He wants to operate on my psyche. His fists are scalpels. He will be my doctor! *Each of these pages is a magic spell.* Things won't go the way of his philosophy if he doesn't put on the shoes I see their pictures, their photographs, and I put them on the floor, stomp on them, spit on them, urinate and defecate on them and worse! The men don't move under your command, put on his father's worn shoes and watch the trucks go by with their sheep and their ugly stink of men, perhaps police officers perhaps just farmers waiting for blood and plebian genes.

The backwards, go.

Your iron hexes are no longer potent against me, Gennaro. There's a floating blob of ectoplasmic hindering me from sealing the envelope containing the invitation to our sensual dismemberment. This bland meaning, bland meaning, bland meaning, bad reviews of bad architectural reports disguised as fiction disguised as an instructional manual printed in Turin. Finally you will get my gift. Finally there will be some gift. You....

Gennaro. My dear, dear Gennaro. You should go outside more often. You should go outside and enjoy the weather, enjoy your neighbors, your friends, you entire village. You should enjoy the life you have at your disposal. You should enjoy yourself more often.

You write these things, these terrible things, in order to both erect and deconstruct the structures around you but we both know THAT THIS IS NOT THE SOLUTION. It is not the answer to your prayers. Do you even pray? I can't imagine you'd have the time. No, not with your writing your philosophy.

So, dear Gennaro, please go outside and enjoy the fresh air and the ground beneath your feet. Please do not count the graves you've created because you'll go dizzy with exhaustion.

My dear love, Gennaro…please….listen and follow me.

I am but a mere structure.

Please do not take me apart. I love you.

You are the only one in the universe.

STRUCTURES II.

BLOCK TIER 1

Gennaro enters the room, enters the piss-poor chamber where he will construct his awful philosophy. After years of blackening the community with his words, Gennaro will build a testament to his ideas. He will form things, awful things.

    ILL-FATED SOLUTIONS, A MAN
NAMED ALDO SQUEEZES
    THE MACHINE AND EXITS WITH INK
EXISTS WITH FIRE

There are scars on his arms where the knives have called upon him. They were village knives, knives born from the blood of his ancestors and the transgressions they have committed in the name of holiness and glorious torment. They were the knives that sprouted from the soil that grew fat with suicides.

    SOME OTHER MOUNTAINS THEY
WERE LOST IN
    TEARS CREEPING FURY THE
MAYOR LOST HIS LIFE

He has ink and he has paper and he has time. Oh, does he have time! He has time to make

maps of his intellect, diagrams of the cold hells of
his lineage. He will strip his mind of distractions
and relinquish control to the brutal airs of his
history, his philosophy.

HOLIDAY OF PURELY BLADES, THE
MAN WON'T MOVE
MEETS RESISTANCE AND DEFLATES
EGO INTO SAND

Gennaro cracks open the bottle filled with bile
and broad strokes of old pens and finally, oh
finally! the lapdogs of the mayor are slit from ear
to ear. Gennaro laughs and pockets the knife.

SEETHING RETURNS SELLING FRUIT
TO DEAD MEN
SOCKS IRONED THROUGH
COBBLESTONE DEVILS

There is a method to Gennaro's fine madness,
some fine black-hearted treatise, a full report of
all that hangs within his prion-riddled brain. Oh,
the brain that pulls beauty out of atrocity! His
fine madness and melancholy alive with the
swelling of insects and rotted fungi! Alone, dear
Gennaro will conquer the space between the body
and the mind!

HORRIBLE MURDERS STRIKE THE
CURRENT SEIZURES

SIGH BETWEEN BEATINGS AND BRUISED HOURS

Gennaro's words are pulled from his teeth, from his mind, from his crackling brain and then, then what? He laughs and pockets the knife! The knife is in his pocket! Do you not understand? Do you not understand the implications of this pure fact? I dare you to ponder this! I dare you to peruse the words that are floating in the air around Gennaro's head!

A
BLOATED LITTLE **HEAD**
POKES OUT
BLEEDS OUT
YOU ARE **THE** ONLY ONE IN
YOUR **UNIVERSE**
THAT
CAN
HEAR
MY VILLAGE
AS IT
IMPLODES
AND SEX DEATH **DRUGS**
TIN FOIL
FOLK SONGS
EAT FALSE UNIVERSE
SLICE 'ER THROAT
PICK **'ER** POCKETS
ISSA GOOD CHOICE
SEE THEE **PRIEST**
PAINTING WALLS
STONE AGE KIDS

BLOCK TIER 2

Gennaro clogs the drain with bits of moon trees. The Etruscan triangles block the passage and Gennaro giggles into the light. He measures the room with the intestines of brittle men! His philosophy is not up for grabs and is not indicative of his childhood. You will not hear about his childhood. You will not hear about his meeting the Watchers or learning the craft of his father. No! Gennaro has no father. He has no mother, no mother but some whore who pulled his rotten bones from the sunken earth of her cunt. That is what Gennaro smells like! That is what he tastes like! And that fills him with joy. Some bottle-fed young philosopher he is not. He is not innocent and he is not a virgin having lost his purity to a slug-covered whore on the beach. She held the aroma of black-hearted saints! How Gennaro inhaled the stench with cosmic pride! Someone told him that the whore was a real devil, a devil from deep in the earth, the caves off the coast. Witches with their long black hair like wet spider webs hocked up from the lungs of children from the village, from the cities far, far north. Gennaro drinks from that bottle, drinks from the bottle from the witches and their old ways, their natural ways, watching the moon as it transforms into wine glasses for mothers and sisters. He clogs the drains with bits of brains and moon trees and Etruscan relics deemed too obscure for the rotting museums. Triangles and giggles in his night philosophy. Oh, the treasures he uncovers in the midst of earth's cunt. He is not innocent but he is not a black-hearted saint. That fills him with joy, this rotten bone cosmos hocked up from witch slugs. Gennaro is so hungry for policeman tongues. He wants to render his fantasies into meat. He is a whore on the beach of philosophical pondering, a devil from deep in the earth, from the bottle, from the wet spider web of the north shaped into triangles and draining into rotted childhoods vomited back into intestinal homesteads. He holds the aroma of black-hearted spirits! He is the climber of moon trees and brittle fathers! He wears masks and hits hammers above the ruins. Things won't go the way of his philosophy if he doesn't put on the dress, put on his faded mother's dress and watch the trucks go by with their chickens and their ugly stink of men, perhaps police officers perhaps just farmers waiting for blood and things. Gennaro doesn't know any songs but if he was to sing one, he imagines he would sing one loud and with a voice he imagines the old priest would have, shouting his prayers and supplications and (in his mind) invocations, evocations, conjuring of old woman spirits and saints for the sake of eating at their ectoplasmic nipples, lunar milk. The chamber opens wide for the solar crocodile, all well and dandy for the man named Gennaro. He worships the terrible skin of that terrible creature, the creature that mocks the very cosmos, the very fabric of the celestial river and with this philosophy, Gennaro will blanket the land with his repulsive words, his deafening mental screams. Things will not get better. Things will get much, much worse and spill the blood of thousands in the caves off the coast, the caves filled with witches and bottles of filthy eyes and spells and teeth but he does not believe in these things, these ugly things because the last thing he wants to do is accept the superstitions of his father and his mother and his brother and sister and long faded shadows blacked out windows and ugly skin he wants to strip off and shade the sky with. Everything is dirty and corrupt within the village and outside of it. He had no energy for anything but his philosophy. He has no energy for anything by some form of hate for every form of life and life's meanings that are splattered through the minds of simple skulls. Blood from wounds squirt sweetly. Into the box with you, Gennaro! You look at me so oddly as if I'd betray your philosophy or betray your somewhat incomplete life in that hospital. Your chamber is filled with spiders and insects and maybe a clown made of morphine. In your dreams you were the target of a Stone Age exorcism. You are a thief, Gennaro! You have stolen my words and my time. You have stolen the smoke from my candle and my mother from the caves! You do not swim so quietly. You do not swim at all! All of your words are false carvings on the walls of my ancestral pyramid full of incestuous blasphemy against crocodile oyster gods but no words for witches shivering in the caves. You wish I'd stop accusing you! You wish I'd stop putting your name to primal pornography. Relax your quivering bones, Gennaro! I'll get to my point in due time. You are afraid to open the doors to my ectoplasmic explanations and your childhood trauma. You say there was no trauma? But I have proof! I have proof that there was childhood trauma! Trauma deep in the blackened neurons of your ugly brain. I have proof! And the proof is this

YOUR COLLECTION BEGINS
WHAT'S WRONG WITH YOUR
PILLOW
DON'T TELL THINGS
TRIANGLES
YOU ARE MESSING WITH
TABLES
YOU ARE MESSING WITH A
VIRUS
YOU ARE **HUMAN**
YOU EAT RAW MEAT
YOU FIT INSIDE THAT BOX
MAYBE YOU COULD PAINT
THE WALLS
YOU HAVE A GOOD IDEA
OF WHAT I WANT

A TRIP UP THE MOUNTAIN

Aldo says, "You worthless bitch!" and slaps the girl across her pale face. He means to torture her. He wants to see her annihilated for no reason other than her insistence on being human.

"Don't you dare call me that!" she says.

"Or what? Or what, you bitch? What are you going to do to me that I already won't do to myself?"

"You're a masochist!"

"Is that a surprise, you little bitch!"

"You call me that again and I'll gut you like your mother gut your father!" she says.

"You are horrible! You wonder why I talk to you like this."

"You talk to me like this because you have no manners."

"Bitch."

"Tarantula."

"I'll kill you someday."

"Don't I know it? Didn't I know it from the first day we met? From the first day we unbridled our passions?"

"And yet you're still here."

"I must be a masochist, too."

"More of a sadist. You love torturing me with your stupidity."

"Beast!"

"Bitch!"

"If you're going to kill me, then just do it. Why should I wait around for it? Why should I waste my time making plans for anything?"

"Because you love the tension. You love this," Aldo says. He digs into his pocket and pulls out a syringe and proceeds to prepare himself for an injection. The drug hits him hard and fast and he sinks into a heartless oblivion, a dirty cry from the village, from the city.

The city with its butchers and rapists. The city with its whores and its children. The city pregnant with abomination after abomination. The drug is like a scalpel that dissects his brain and leaves it for the dogs. The dogs of the city are rabid. They are infested with syphilis and solar poisoning. They are the light bulbs that lead Aldo out into the city, into the buildings that spell disaster. Aldo dines at the coffee house, just simple coffee and rolls, bread that soaks up the substances in his stomach and his digestion is excellent. His ears ring and his belly rumbles and he belches out into the coffee house and the people around him applaud for they think it is one of Aldo's famous poems, the poems he writes down for the women around the city.

Oh, Horus, oh simple man enlightened with a handful of papers showing Cippus and crocodile buffoons. Because you love the tension, dear love! Because you love the tension!

MAHES
NUN
HER PRIMEVAL
MOUND
RAET-TAWY
SOME TUSCAN
BEAKED CLOWN

THIS EPISODE
ENDS
AT 22 MINUTES

pause the machine
east fish

777 ARADIA

There were always clowns, yes, clowns that battled our ancestors, slaughtered them when the time was right (which means, when the moon was right) and we were all birthed in some sort of lunar abattoir, a slick remnant of our eternal stregheria. Who came with us? La Befana? We blamed ourselves for the mirrors.

Sometimes I like the cold and sometimes the cold makes me think of clowns and their Great Mother, the one with the gargantuan breasts that sit on the pyramidal mounds of corn. They dance, they sing and dance and figure out ways to torment us through the walls and through the transmissions from the old war. They even tampered with our automobiles, those relics of our prosperity that are now all just reminders of our social impotence.

I remember driving my mother's car into the field and praying for some sort of return to the earth. What kind of return could I have hoped for? Maybe a return to the hollowness inside? Certainly the planet is hollow. Certainly it is inhabited by those small men I've read about in my mother's journals. They sing to certain people, they sing songs and bring so much to them in the corners of mirrors, where you could almost see them.

There were always clowns drawn above my father's bed and I wondered why he had to look at clowns in order to make love to my mother unless the clowns were drawn for my mother to look at but even that was strange and I could not and cannot get over that fact, the looking at clowns as one makes love, some smiles within the passion.

One of the clowns, I swear to it, looked like the embodiment of Pan, circling the Goat Star, Hircus, but it's all nonsense, I'm sure. No clown looks like that. No clown scratched in the wooden walls of my father's room where he impregnating my mother, gave her rotten sperm from his alcoholic testicles, spitting viper's venom out of the Lare's house and into the rotting earthen shed.

I stand as one man as the epitome of calm mirror images, tampering with the seals of medicines in the stores, putting poison into innocent home remedies, oh, and that is my only sin, I assure you!

They dance and sing under the moon with their robes bleeding out like those goddamn soldiers who came into the village and raped the young men with dicks and sticks and filthy rags lit on fire and sprayed with weaponized liquid until the village boys turned into deformed clowns and crippled displays of perversion and ever since then they cannot stop masturbating into the cows' mouths and the communal wells we all use but we don't blame them for that because it was the soldiers, the soldiers, the goddamn war that brought upon us this carnival of hemlock and honey.

THE FROG SHOWS ON THE IVORY WAND

My house is on the corner. It is next to a farm that no longer grows crops or raises animals. It is not much of a farm.

My house is in poor condition. It is only a few years from collapsing into a heap by which time I will surely be deceased. I do not count myself lucky when it comes to life. Certain structures I've erected have come back to haunt me and the blueprints I kept safe are now scattered to the wind.

My house is also my burial chamber.

I am but a simple structure caught in a complex plan created by a simple god who does not know that structures can't mix.

I used to be a farmer but now I am not.

Now I am just a man.

Now I am just.

ON THE BACK OF A SODA CAN:

The Opener of the Ways has let ANTONIO fly towards heaven amongst his brothers, the structures. ANTONIO has moved his arms as a sun-crocodile, he has beaten his scaled wings like a kite. He flies up, he who flies up, ye men. ANTONIO flies up away from you.

It has come to my attention that some sources (who will remain unknown though I know how suspicious that is) have degraded me in their periodicals and despite my attempts to blockade any and all rumors, misinformation, and outright lies, I am left at the mercy of scoundrels and men of low morality who want nothing more than to see me dead or hanging from a crane in one of their precious pits where they play with cement all day and all night regardless of weather or health of the workers who, I might add, are withheld from getting the necessary amount of food, water, and healthcare that are basic to the survival of the species despite the lack of survival throughout the surrounding villages, the villages that have come under constant scrutiny because of their unorthodox rituals involving the exposure of their citizens to contaminated soil which has, as of last year, caused fifty-five deaths among those aged twenty years or younger, and eighty-five deaths among those aged twenty-one years or older which also includes those people who only live in the village part time as many often work in the surrounding towns doing menial work for poverty-pay and that is an unacceptable way of life, in my most humble opinion despite the suspicions put upon me by nefarious sources (who will remain unknown and nameless despite my having their photographs in my possession). My name was Antonio Magogoli and I used to be the husband of Angelina De Luca, sister of Aldo De Luca. I used to own a gun but now I simply use my finger. I point to the intended victim and they are half-dead as he stands and fully dead by the time he goes to bed. My partners, veterans of some Hong Kong perversion cult of gangsters, assist me and I am eternally grateful though slightly repulsed. Like I said my name used to be Antonio Magogoli but now I am simply called other words, no words, just gestures.

ATI CATH
THIS IS YOUR LAST
NOTICE, CHELPHUN

DO NOT TURN THE
PAGE
UNTIL YOU'VE
COMPLETED
ALL
RITUALS

ENLIGHTENED
BASTARDS
OV THEE
FICKLE LIGHT

Cruising Glimpse

There are rituals inherent in structures, simple structures, complex structures, all structures alive or dead, beautiful or ugly, calm or anxious, shoved into dust, those cement structures and structures made of playing cards and popsicle sticks. A genetic and cultural conflict boards the train from here to Palermo but...there is no train!

I have met with men on trains and have divulged the secrets concerning all structures and have even let the men get a glimpse of my book, my journal documenting structures and their curses.

Everyone knows the sodomites run the villages down south. What a cesspool of laws and liberation all twisted into semen-stained ropes hanging from cranes and overlooking their cement structures, giving the villagers something to look at when they are raped with drugs and witch-wine, bottles of clear depravity fermented from the testicles of sullen men, eight-hundred-proof and all with conspiracies of local elections, those bastard sodomites!

The storekeepers do not welcome me into their pitiful shops because I have revealed their wares to be empty tokens of an empty society. They are all wretched! They are empty but refuse to embrace the fact! I am therefore the creature of their hateful arousal. I make movies to reveal my sexuality, lighting small farmhouses on fire, shooting feral cats and eating rabid dogs, meal fit for a king but I am no king, only a rabid example of your beautiful capitalism and sodomy. I am a product of it! I am a product of that partnership. I used to build structures but now...now I am such a structure! I am nothing! I am everything! Glimpse my curse!

PACHA
Goes
Shopping
And
Picks up a silk suit
At
Selvansl Tularias
It fits him quite nicely
In the nighttime
PACHA
Will commit acts of rape
In the countryside
He is a deviant beyond
All deviance
He thinks
Rimbaud was a bore
But don't we all
Burning his ugly papers
PACHA
Relives it all
And comes close to
SUICIDE
As well

The diagnosis, of course, was more severe than I had expected. 'He is, no doubt, mentally ill,' they had told me. I didn't believe them. I *couldn't* believe them. My dear son could not be sick in that way, in the way that there is no cure for him, no matter what pills or potions or rest they prescribe, I know there is no cure for what they deem to be 'mental illness' in their little offices surrounded by dusty but untouched textbooks explaining all the maladies of the human condition. God! 'He is, no doubt, mentally ill,' is what they said but I believe what they wanted to say was, 'Give up now and you'll have at least a few years left of peace,' but they just didn't have the courage to say it. So I stood there hearing this diagnosis and knew that it was my fault for my genetic material was, no doubt, sub par. My very was full of ugly proteins and acids and invisible prions and satanic nucleotides. I had passed it all down to him and he was to suffer this 'illness' that was really a cosmic curse that strikes those who are descendents of the first village, the first sick people in the desert, on the mountains, in the hills, in the caves, writing on the stone walls, eating roots and seeing visions, telling the other villagers about those visions, causing dreams, causing a culture to form, shaping attitudes, routines of sex, commerce, astronomical contradictions, and then now this 'mental illness' I can't escape from but I am not 'mentally ill' nor am I at all ill in any shape or form despite my passing along something to my son. God! I'm not what everyone thinks. I'm not a contagious monster. The diagnosis, of course, was more severe than I had expected but what did I expect, really but a diagnosis that would tell me that everything would be okay and my son would be well in only a few weeks after some honest to goodness medicine but I couldn't believe them when they told me it was some sort of 'mental illness' because, let's face it, that phrase has no meaning, it has not structure. It has not real structure at all. It's a building made of thought and fog, nothing really, so the diagnosis was useless to me and I wasted time arguing with the doctors about the language they used and the implications and the future of not only my son but of me because I had no real comprehension of what 'mentally ill' meant in terms of human beings. Was it also a spiritual illness? Was there something in the actual brain that was wrong or was it just a problem with habits and routines? Did I damage my son by instilling conflicting values or habits? Was his perspectives skewed in some sort of ill way? I imagined this and I still imagine it and I still regret not being able to win all of the arguments I had with the doctors but you cannot win arguments with doctors because they are the ones with the degrees and training and power and they will always insist that one is overreacting especially a parent of a patient to which they will say, 'You're overreacting' and that's it, you can't do anything about it except ask questions that will be answered only in tiny dribs and drabs and complicated medical language or condescending baby talk. The doctors do not see mere men as equals so therefore they cannot explain things and so I had no idea what it meant to be 'mentally ill' until I talked to my son and he explained everything. Then I understood. I understood everything.

Aldo's day in court.

He pleaded to the judge. The judge did not want to listen or rather, he did not want to believe that Aldo was telling the truth even though (as was discovered later) he was indeed telling the truth. Aldo did not commit the crimes he was being accused of committing despite it appearing like he was the main culprit in a multitude of gruesome and immoral actions.

Gennaro was in court as well, giving "support" to his ex-brother-in-law because he knew the man was innocent. How did he know this? He knew this because *he* had been the one to commit the crimes! And now in diabolical arousal, he watched Aldo be condemned by the judge, that heartless judge (Gennaro wished a curse on the judge. At least give an accused man a chance at freedom!)

The verdict.

Guilty on all accounts.

Aldo's sisters and wife and mother and grandmother all collapse and cry and yell for the judge to rethink his decision and when they saw that he was ignoring them, they cursed him to some a dark hell full of whore stench and sickness. Yes! They hated the judge even more than Aldo did.

ILL-FATED
SOLUTIONS, A
MAN NAMED ALDO
SQUEEZES
THE MACHINE AND
EXITS WITH INK
EXISTS WITH FIRE
ALSO
ALDO
IN SHACKLES
WRITES BOOKS

TIER 9

Reading through a book, I see a picture of a camel and I have the urge to rip the animal apart and devour it, not out of a desire for sustenance but out of pure hate for that satanic desert creature, the camel, that ugly thing. God! I read through a book and spit on the picture of the camel for I cannot simply bring the animal to life so it can be victim of my teeth and nails so I desecrate its image just as I desecrate the images of men and women alike throughout my life. I see their pictures, their photographs, and I put them on the floor, stomp on them, spit on them, urinate and defecate on them and worse! I do things that God closes His eyes to because He knows it would corrupt even Him. He doesn't stop me, no, He doesn't stop me because He knows it is out of my own Free Will that I do these things and He created this Free Will or rather, He allowed this Free Will to reign in the hearts and souls of ugly men like myself so He closes His eyes and thinks of pure things while I desecrate the images of men and women who arouse my hateful pineal gland.

Last night, Gennaro dreamt of a camel. The animal was standing in front of him in the desert. They were the only living things for miles until a herd of sheep ran through the scene and large black ships shaped like smiles flew through the air. Gennaro kicked the camel and the animal spoke to him in fluid French. Gennaro couldn't understand the thing. He kicked it again and the sand gave way and a storm created a face shaped like the camel only larger and more sinister looking. A caravan of sick men road up behind Gennaro and asked him if he was willing to sell the camel for they were hungry for camel meat and wanted to devour the thing from front to back and were willing to pay a good price for the beast. Gennaro told the men that he wasn't even sure it was his camel but that he'd be willing to part with it for just some water and maybe a few minutes with the most attractive of the men. One of the men (the youngest) agreed to spend some time with Gennaro and the other men took the camel while Gennaro and the young man sat on the desert sand and started exploring each other's bodies with hand and tongue and finally cock until the camel was slaughtered at which time both men ejaculated into each other's palms after which they drank water and feasted on camel meat and Gennaro awoke with his tongue lapping up the green water on the stone floor.

THE POLITICAL SITUATION INSIDE BERNHARD PROVINCE

It is not a simple task to sum up the events that led to the dissolution of the Bernhard Province. Many writers more intelligent than I have tried (and failed) to come up with an accurate chronology of the events. This isn't from any fault of their own but is a result of the intricacy and chaotic nature of the province itself. Both the physical landscape as well as the cultural and political structures were based upon a primitive mythology that was not overtly recognized among the populous and only that fact only manifested itself after the discovery of the personal papers of Sansone D'Antona. It was after that discovery that the true structure of Bernhard Province came to light.

Gennaro, that papal hound, that worshipper of an antiquated Dagon, the pitiful writer of rumors and insidious gossip…he sits alone in his chamber, contemplating the philosophies of ugly reputations.

There are scars on his torso where the village wives called their knives upon him. They were blades born from the blood of sea caves. They birthed transgressions committed in the name of holiness and glorious torment along the shore. They were the knives that sprouted from the soil that grew fat with homicides that may or may not have been associated with organized crime.

Gennaro wishes to slit throats in his dreams. He wishes to watch the dream-blood ooze in that special way one only sees in dreams…the slow oozing…the slow movement that tingles the body and relieves the mind of all tension and worry. He wishes to slaughter indiscriminately because that's what his philosophy calls for…even in dreams. Yes, even in dreams.

He writes and writes and yet…he never does not feel satisfied.

All the people lit fires of figures, all semi-human but all also totally unlike their counterparts even with the fish markets being what they are, with all the clams and oysters and semi-fresh fish, enlightened eaters, all the priests who shop and try to get their fish for free because their boss is the boss and fish should be free, god knows it, and so all of us lose some of our value, just semi-human rungs on a black ladder.

....

I beg to differ, Gennaro. You will not convince me. You will not convince me like you've convinced my comrades. They are ignorant men, ignorant swine, sons of festering whores, of ugly and dying soldiers, and I am not them. So you cannot convince me, you cannot put your stamp onto my soul. You own soul smell likes the inside of satan's fish market, dirty and eternally evil and pungent and you will not bring me into it. No, Gennaro, you will not. I beg to differ.

PACHA
Shopping
In the countryside
And
As well
Selvansl Tularias
Goes
In the nighttime
PACHA
He is a deviant beyond
Picks up a silk suit
At
All deviance
He thinks
Rimbaud was a bore
But don't we all
Burning his ugly papers
Will commit acts of rape
PACHA
Relives it all
And comes close to
SUICIDE
It fits him quite nicely

Gennaro enters the room, enters the piss-poor chamber where he will construct his awful philosophy. After years of blackening the community with his words, Gennaro will build a testament to his ideas. He will form things, awful things. He will author volumes of his vile philosophy. He will blanket the world with his mania.

There comes a time in each generation when one individual must vent their grievances and grief and dissatisfaction and spiritual anger and lustful anguish in the form of the written word.

Gennaro sings black-hearted hymns and offers up his skin.

There are scars on his arms where the knives called upon him. They were village knives, knives born from the blood of his ancestors and the transgressions they have committed in the name of holiness and glorious torment. They were the knives that sprouted from the soil that grew fat with suicides.

Men, women, children…all were victims of Gennaro's elaborate suicidal purge. He has collected their death masks and has taken photographs of their mouths as they whispered their last words, their last shot at entering the heaven of their village's god. Oh, and Gennaro loves those last words. How sweet they are in the grey matter of his awful brain!

He has ink and he has paper and he has time. Oh, does he have time. He has time to make maps of his intellect, diagrams of the cold hells of his lineage. He will strip his mind of distractions and relinquish control to the brutal airs of his history, his philosophy.

The ink has been harvested from the veins of the village harlot. It has been harvested from the obsidian rain that falls over the village orphanage. It has been harvested from the candles that stand guard over the village's black masses. It is the ink of fallen faces…and of death. Gennaro cracks open the bottle filled with bile and broad strokes of old pens and finally, oh finally, the lapdogs of the mayor are slit from ear to ear. Gennaro laughs and pockets the knife.

He enjoys the feel of the weapon in his pocket. It hums against his leg. It hums in the dead language of murdered children. Gennaro hums along with the knife and remembers cracked teeth and bloated gums.

There is a method to Gennaro's fine madness, some fine black-hearted treatise, a full report of all that hangs within his prion-riddled brain. Oh, the brain that pulls beauty out of atrocity! His fine madness and melancholy alive with the swelling of insects and rotted fungi! Alone, dear Gennaro will conquer the space between the body and the mind!

And he does it for you. He does it for you, the reader of obscene books. He does it for you, teller of gruesome tales. He does it for you, violator of machines. He does it for you, father of the disturbed and mother of the crippled. He does it for the universe, that brittle and corrupting whore.

Gennaro's words are pulled from his teeth, from his mind, from his crackling brain and then, then what? He laughs and pockets the knife! The knife is in his pocket! Do you not understand? Do you not understand the implications of this pure fact? I dare you to ponder this! I dare you to peruse the words that are floating in the air around Gennaro's head!

The knife is *not* the knife!

Gennaro's hands are *not* his hands!

Gennaro's words are *not* his words!

Gennaro is *not* Gennaro!

THIS IS A
PAGE
IN A BOOK

(LEAVE PAGE
BLANK)

((elongate philosophy))

Some of our sons teach Hebrew at the university. It wasn't our decision and we made it clear we disapprove of their academic endeavors. Academics! Can you believe such an area to focus on in this world of earthly and carnal delights? Our sons should know the best life has to offer…and the worst. They occupy an intellectual void. They don't listen to their elders. We are left home to twaddle and destroy anything and everything, our dreams and illusions of black glass, those buildings we dream of and the buildings we drive by on our way to the slaughter pits, the houses of pungent blood and menstrual fascination. We aren't light bulbs, you fools! Some of our sons think we are

IMAGINARY

And they may be right

May 1, 2112

Dear Sir/Madam/Other,

Contrary to popular believe you me I don't recognize the problematic in determination the systematic behaviorist theorem in regarding my last opportunist offering to your.

I regretful to reform you that our last meet was a mistaken in terming of successful properties of development the lasting structuring reformist spectral lining forced.

This classifying locus concerned the blackening methodical placements accomplished many models with myriad occupying regarding procedural plotting laments.

Obvious I would liken to recording all futuristic meet in case of misinterpretation concerns and confused. All fish coincide, a loss of earring capital will no doubtful reinforcements our upcoming yearly.

Hour structures have been structurally sounded grown lightheaded. Till then weave consequences ourselves inhumanly.

Yours,

Antonio Magogoli

The housing project is the only structure I liked in the entire city of Turin. The cement and glass structure is known as **LOLLOBRIGIDA** and was named after the actress Gina Lollobrigida. It was built in 1968 by Renato Questi, an architect and entrepreneur from Florence. Questi originally made his fortune publishing religious tracts in Slavic. He became an architect after having seen Marco Bertolucci's 1959 film *STRUCTURES*.

LOLLOBRIGIDA is a refuge for me. It is the only structure I can stomach in my post-war life. I do not have an apartment here but I sleep in the hallways. I eat in them, too. This is after I dig in the rubbish bins for food. I often go into the basement to take drugs and watch my illuminated thoughts play out with asbestos and rats. I sing songs I've learned when I worked with Armand on his boat. We used harvest the vile oysters that coated the shallow sea floor.

I'd like to die in **LOLLOBRIGIDA** and I probably will someday. I take far too many drugs to survive and I'm positive that the illuminated rats will come take me away and dissect me. They will use my parts to build a new heaven and a new earth, a new structure for all the people who die in their squalid apartments in the cement and glass structure known as **LOLLOBRIGIDA**.

Gennaro throws marbles against the wall and wishes for them to turn into eyes, small child-eyes, tiny mirrors to the future but he's left disappointed for they are *not* child-eyes, they are *not* tiny mirrors to the future. They are simply marbles.

His philosophy is done, almost done, and is a book full of blank verses. He despises the structures of books, of words, everything and anything with some form. He hates and he loves them and knows they will destroy him.

Those words he scrawled into his mother's white and purple body, he squeezed the last remaining remarks from her throat and rendered her useless in the scheme of things.

Finally relenting, his father tied a rope around his pitiful organs and splattered something fierce across the field, the one where the priest had violated that slave.

Gennaro eats the marbles and hopes for the worst of things.

He always hopes for the worst.

HORRIBLE MURDERS STRIKE THE
CURRENT SEIZURES SIGH
BETWEEN BEATINGS AND
BRUISED HOURS SOME OTHER
MOUNTAINS THEY WERE LOST IN
TEARS CREEPING FURY THE
MAYOR LOST HIS LIFE IN
PAINFUL PROSE DEAR LORDS
AND LADIES AND THOSE AREN'T
GAMES, MY DEAR FELLOWS,
WITHOUT KNIVES OF MOUNTAIN
CLIMBERS AND HOISTING UP
RUINS FOR J. PARSON'S
ABORTIONS IN ROME
EVERYTHING FEELS PURPLE
STRAINED AND SPRAINED LOST
TO THE EPIDEMIC OF STRIKING
TURTLE SHORES IN THE
RESTAURANT ATE WITH
MISTRESS AND BOTTLED UP
BOXES WE'RE NOT PRINTING THE
LAST OF HIS WORDS WE ARE NOT
PRINTING THE LAST OF HIS EVIL
VILE PHILOSOPHY WE DO NOT
SUPPORT ANY WORDS AND OH

THOSE 'ORRIBLE 'URDERS OV 'UMOUR AND BLACK LICE SAINTHOOD BLEEDING BIRTHDEATH AND DAMNED MOTHERHOOD WITHOUT WHICH WE WOULD NOT HAVE THIS SUCH PHILOSOPHY RETURNING OURSELVES TO THE GARAGE OF OUR PITIFUL SPITTING AND TOILET TRAINING IN THE MIDST OF THE VILLAGE PRAYERS LIKENED TO DUST AND TRIANGLE HANDS RIPPER TRADE STREET ROUGH THINGS

STRUCTURALLY UNSOUND

Gennaro's words are pulled from his teeth, from his mind, from his crackling brain and then, then what? He laughs and pockets the knife! The knife is in his pocket! Do you not understand? Do you not understand the implications of this pure fact? I dare you to ponder this! I dare you to peruse the words that are floating in the air around Gennaro's head!

I stand as one man as the epitome of calm mirror images, tampering with the seals of medicines in the stores, putting poison into innocent home remedies, oh, and that is my only sin, I assure you!

You look at me so oddly as if I'd betray your philosophy or betray your somewhat incomplete life in that hospital. Your chamber is filled with spiders and insects and maybe a clown made of morphine. In your dreams you were the target of a Stone Age exorcism. You are a thief, Gennaro! You have stolen my words and my time. You have stolen the smoke from my candle and my mother from the caves! You do not swim so quietly. You do not swim at all!

There are rituals inherent in structures, simple structures, complex structures, all structures alive or dead, beautiful or ugly, calm or anxious, shoved into dust, those cement structures and structures made of playing cards and popsicle sticks. A genetic and cultural conflict boards the train from here to Palermo but…there is no train!

There were always clowns drawn above my father's bed and I wondered why he had to look at clowns in order to make love to my mother unless the clowns were drawn for my mother to look at but even that was strange and I could not and cannot get over that fact, the looking at clowns as one makes love, some smiles within the passion.

And he does it for you. He does it for you, the reader of obscene books. He does it for you, teller of gruesome tales. He does it for you, violator of machines. He does it for you, father of the disturbed and mother of the crippled. He does it for the universe, that brittle and corrupting whore.

I am but a simple structure caught in a complex plan created by a simple god who does not know that structures can't mix.

I used to be a farmer but now I am not.

Now I am just a man.

Now I am just a structure.

III.

That fickle light bringer, says Joseph the Bastard Son. You know his leader, the man named Aldo De Luca, cousin of Marco Del Duca, and father of the infamous man known simply as *"THE INMOST HOST."*

I know where you can find these men. (Find these men and kill these men!) They hide out in the back room of the shop called BOUTH & EFFEMINATE. I've been there. I know many of you have been there. It is a den of weak vipers. The birthplace of Poor Jim, that cowardly cuckold!

There are splendid rituals inherent in splendorous structures, simple structures, complex structures, all structures alive or dead, beautiful or ugly, calm or anxious, shoved into dust, those cement structures and structures made of playing cards and matchsticks, twigs and blocks, idols and fermented fruit. Your lemon tree is for the hangman, the limp-wristed hangman who spills candy from the gut and builds puppets in the attic of the Milligan Lady.

You turn your radio into an instrument... for torturous intent!

I have met with men on roads and have divulged the secrets concerning all structures and have opened my EARS for them. They insert knives into my codes. They insert blades into my playful manikin train birds. They insert coins into my eye sockets and fish out false bruises that color in books fresh from the bakery.

The folk songs of my village are haunting odes to the Stone Age perversions of my mechanical ancestors. You are the only one in the penultimate universe. Eat the false toy block moon. Drink wine unearthed from the farm. The stench of cosmic pride. Your intestinal homesteads relieve you and pocket the spoils of the shopping center. You wear masks and make noise. Sing your songs but don't worry. I AM RECOVERING OKAY. The solar crocodile opens wide. WITH RESPECT. He eats and talks French and he is the surgeon! He wants to render his fantasies into abstract meat. He is a whore on the beach of philosophical posturing, a devil from deep in the earth, from the bottle, from the wet spider web of the north shaped into rectangles and draining into bloated childhoods vomited back into political art of his elderly years.

Things won't go the way of his philosophy if he doesn't put on the shirt, put on his father's worn shirt and watch the trains go by with their goats and their ugly stink of women, perhaps police officers perhaps just farmers waiting for blood and popular genes.

Things will not get better, dear Gennaro. Things will get much, much worse and spill the blood of millions in the caves off the coast, the caves filled with witches and bottles of filthy lungs and spells and teeth but we do not believe in these things, these ugly things because the last thing we want to do is accept the superstitions of our fathers and long faded shadows blacking out windows and ugly skin we want to strip off and shade the sky with. Gennaro doesn't deserve us.

Aldo will be left raped and murdered under a brazen sky made of lung!

Everything is dirty and corrupt within the village and outside of it. We have no energy for anything but our silly philosophy. Juice from wounds shower us.

Into the cave with you, Gennaro!

You look at me so oddly as if I'd betray your philosophy or betray your somewhat incomplete life in that 'hospital'. What a 'hospital' it is!

All the nurses molest you. All the doctors examine you with their spidery fingers and metallic instruments. They fill out charts in cuneiform and call upon your parents to tell them the terrible news.

Gennaro is contagious!

Pepper sprung ghosts along the road with tables with no chance to plot the long headed murders in the books. What books? What books, you say? We don't know, you traitorous worm!

A leaky flip runs flippant around the structured bogs while doomsday cogs **explode possum** dust through the highways of motion sickness chimpanzees.

Blackbirds bit the king (Gennaro) and outlasted the entire population of **singing stars and costumed Greeks who fought against** playful librarians who check me in and check me out and read me to the children like ugly puppet tales (Punch and Boothie). Everything is a moment NOW and not from some universal source.

Animals make ugly animal sounds through lemon tree horns.

Someone built structures out of toy blocks and left them here for me to clean up. I am appalled but not surprised. I AM VERY SURPRISED. I do not have disgust for anything BUT YOU but you know that because you have seen my murderous rage when I pulled my knife from my coat and held it up to your skinny effeminate neck and said, 'You disgust me just as much as you disgust yourself!' but I did not harm you because to harm you is to give you the satisfaction of winning my passion even if only venomous passion.

Gennaro was born in one of the poorer villages south of here. **HE WAS BORN VERY MUCH LIKE A NORMAL INFANT EXCEPT THAT HE WAS GENNARO.**

The exact village is unknown, of course, since the villages down there keep no records for births or deaths and Gennaro himself would not divulge that information to anyone. **I'VE TRIED TO FIND OUT BUT HAVE ALWAYS BEEN MET WITH DISDAIN AND REFUSAL.**

I do know he was born in one of the poorest of villages. His mother was most likely a prostitute who worked the beach, waiting for the fishermen to come in. His father, from what I know, was unemployed but made some money selling secondhand newspapers. **HIS PARENTS ARE REALLY INCONSEQUENTIAL TO OUR STORY AND TO ANYONE'S STORY.**

Gennaro's childhood was spent helping his father dig through trash as well as taunting the other village children. He was a well-known thief and firebug by the time he was twelve years old though no one sought any formal charges against him seeing that his mother was a prostitute and his father was a pathetic example of a parental figure. In fact, most of the villagers felt sorry for poor Gennaro. **WHO WOULD NOT FEEL SORRY FOR THIS SORRY HUMAN BEING? POOR GENNARO HADN'T HAD A CHANCE TO BECOME FULLY HUMAN.**

A TURN FOR THE WORST.

There is such thing as 'too much agitation' and that leads me to my next point. I think your refusal to accept or even acknowledge my proposal to illuminate the man we know as Adolfo Goines is an uninformed decision to say the least. I'm not suggesting you sacrifice or ignore your conscience but I do insist you rethink your plan to thwart my plans of illumination. You will not succeed. That is something I can promise you. You will not succeed in blocking my actions or in murdering me. Oh, you didn't think I'd have the courage to broach the subject, eh? I do! I've always had the courage. You have underestimated me from the beginning. Too much agitation, indeed! I am agitated as we speak! Adolfo deserves what I want to give him and if you cannot see that, well, then you are as blind as your grandmother! Do you actually think I will relent? Do you think I will just give up because you use those precious skills you've learned at the university? Oh, I will not give up. And I will not be murdered! At least not by the likes of you. No!

1974 BROADCAST NARRATION:

Rompiamo lontano dalle nostre cose infantili.

Anche con la nostra testa in materia adulti, a volte sentiamo il bisogno di scavare nel nostro passato, nelle nostre visioni cavernosi e ritualizzate di apocalissi paterni. Seething rage flock. Sì, anche Gennaro prenderà parte nel nostro esorcismo psicologico.

Vicino alla stazione di servizio c'è una libreria piena di calcare tomi arcaici. Quali sono questi libri su? Io non conosco le specifiche, ma ho sentito voci su sigilli pallidi brutti e necromanzia architettonica. A pocket of your eyeballs.

Non c'è stupidità peggiore della morte.

Rompiamo lontano dai nostri pensieri e le routine infantili. Farò ancora niente, io ripeterò niente, riceverò nulla.

Non c'è nulla per te, ragazzino senza un lavoro o una macchina o di un fidanzato.

Un diavolo in abiti femminili, un piccolo modo femminile di fare le cose, fiori e tatuaggi.

Gennaro vuole tagliare gole nei suoi sogni. Avete mai sognato?

Vuole vedere il melma sogno di sangue in quel modo speciale si vede solo nei sogni ... too many spiders stillicidio lento ... il movimento lento che pizzica il corpo e allevia la mente di ogni tensione e preoccupazione. Ti capita mai di preoccuparsi?

Egli vuole massacrare indiscriminatamente perché è quello che la sua filosofia chiede ... anche nei sogni. Sì, anche nei sogni. Pensi che i sogni penis sono premonizioni? Credi che i sogni sono importanti per l'anima di una persona?

Gennaro scrive e scrive, eppure ... lui mai non si sente soddisfatto. **Automobiles and strict nannies.** Ma chi è mai veramente soddisfatto? Chi ha davvero mai si sente contenuto in questa vita? Nessuno! Nessuno si sente di contenuti e così quando mi dici ti senti così soddisfatto, so che sei un bugiardo!

Tagliamo al cuore della questione, va bene?

Sei una donna.

Sei un diavolo.

Ti conosco bene nella toilette di questa fabbrica guerra bulbo oculare. Io sono un ladro morente. Io sono un uomo popolare. **Metallic livers.** Le macchine corrono in coperte sogno e brillanti dita di fuoco.

E 'stato raccolto dalle candele che si ergono a guardia messe nere del villaggio. È l'inchiostro di facce caduti ... e di morte. Lo fa per voi, il lettore di libri osceni. Mi permetto di dissentire, Gennaro. Non mi convince. Non mi convincermi che tu hai convinto i miei compagni. Sono uomini ignoranti, suina ignoranti, figli di puttane purulente, di soldati brutti e morenti, e io non sono loro. Quindi non mi può convincere, non si può mettere il timbro sulla mia anima. **Ungodly pumps.** È proprio odore anima gradite all'interno del mercato del pesce di satana, sporco e eternamente il male e pungente e non mi mettono in esso. No, Gennaro, non lo farai. Mi permetto di dissentire. Lo fa per voi, narratore di storie raccapriccianti. Lo fa per voi, violatore delle macchine. Lo fa per voi, padre della disturbato e madre di storpi e malati e ultraterrena. Lo fa per l'universo, quella solid feces puttana fragile e corruttore. Gennaro lancia biglie contro il muro e desidera per loro si trasformano in occhi, piccoli bambini-occhi, piccoli specchi per buttons trees labia folds il futuro, ma ha lasciato deluso perché non sono bambini-occhi, non sono piccoli specchi per il futuro. Sono semplicemente marmi. Non marmi sono semplici. Marmi sono gli occhi.

MARMI SONO GLI OCCHI!

DEFINITIONS//////

Structures are ideally objects that are partially manmade and partially a result of some ill-gotten epiphenomenon. As I write this I am staring off out the window while also gazing at the pile of books on my desk as well as picking a scab on my leg. I end this documentation by reminding you, the reader, that you not only disgust **me** but you disgust **yourself**. That is the worst crime.

You are a criminal.

You are no better than those manmade structures I abhor.

Be gone with you!

Be a ghost for me now!

Gennaro will find you.

He will slit your throat.

He will then transform into a giraffe.

A black giraffe!

Oh, such bitter words for you.

But this is the end.

My dear disgusting reader.